KU-268-036

The 108th Sheep

Ayano Imai

BLOOMSBURY
CHILDREN'S
BOOKS

Nimitz couldn't sleep a wink. This was very puzzling as she had never had trouble sleeping before, even after the most exciting day. She tried everything she could think of, but nothing made her feel sleepy.

She drank milk, she read books, but they only made her more wide awake. Then she had an excellent idea.

"I'll count sheep!" she thought. "That will make me fall asleep. By the time I count to ten, I'll be nodding off!"

But Nimitz counted to ten … and then to twenty … and before she knew it, she'd reached 100!

"There goes 106," she went on. "And there's 107. And now it must be …"

There was a thud, and the bed shook slightly. But the 108th sheep did not appear.

Nimitz stepped neatly out of bed to see what was wrong. And behind the headboard she found the 108th sheep, flat on the floor, with a large bump on his forehead.

"I can't do it!" he bleated miserably.

"I've been training hard like all the other sheep," he whimpered, "but I've never been able to jump very high. And I certainly can't jump over *your* bed." And the 108th sheep looked very sad indeed.

"It's all very unfortunate," said the 109th sheep, pushing forward. "If 108 doesn't jump over your bed, Nimitz, then none of us can get any sleep. And we're so tired!"

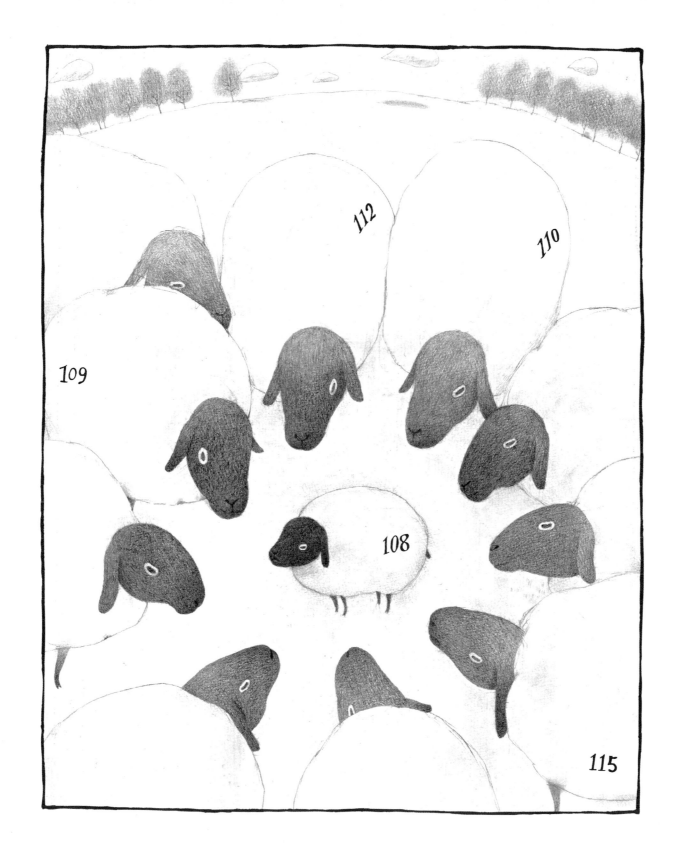

"Well," cried Nimitz, "we must simply help 108 to jump higher!"
So she and the sheep tried every idea they could think of ...

But nothing seemed to help the 108th sheep.

"There's only one thing for it, then," said Nimitz, and she started to make a large hole in the headboard.

All the sheep, from 109 to infinity, held their breath. The 108th sheep took a running jump. Up, up, up he soared, bleating hopefully as he went.

Down, down, down towards the hole he flew …

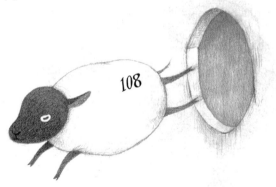

… and slipped through, landing safely on the other side.

Gratefully, everyone curled up and fell asleep.

Nimitz awoke the next morning
after sleeping a wonderful, peaceful sleep.
The hole in the headboard had gone.
The sheep in her bed had also gone.
   "I think I will always sleep well from
now on," said Nimitz, smiling to herself.

And the 108th sheep knew that she was
right.

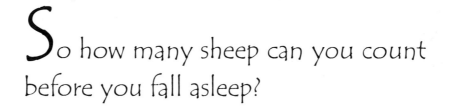

So how many sheep can you count before you fall asleep?

And can you find the 108th sheep?

104